DROWNING IN MY OWN POTENTIAL

DROWNING IN MY OWN POTENTIAL

THOUGHTS AND POEMS

MADISON DAKIN

For my grandfather, Bolo.
Para mi abuelo, Bolo.

intro

this book epiphanies,
this book a piece of me;
real
and
raw
and
true.
in penning this,
i hope to take my light
and shine it on the misunderstanding,
voice the emotions as my soul knows true,
embrace my role of
a buoy in treacherous waters
for those who can no longer swim.
this book the hopeful unveiling of
the strenuous morph we undergo
through pressure;
rocks yield diamonds,
but what am i?
through change i grow,
yet still victim to time.
when doubts and hopes
make bets inside us
i pray reality wins.
so shall we,
drape intricately interwoven quilts
of reality upon us,
and shed our lights on
a piece of us,
a piece of you and me.
this book partly a testimony to you,
i hope you know who you are.

a language only we speak

i have sat down to write about you on many occasions,
but through many attempts i've failed.
countless drafts about you lie within the
jet black ink
on the tinted yellow pages
of my little red notebook.
i'll admit, i am stubborn in my ways, always have been.
i refuse to publish anything short of the perfection you radiate.
but i sit here, writing this, at an ultimatum,
for i cannot
not
write
about you.
but writing that inadequately represents your
natural perfection
is pointless to me.

but perfection is impossible, you'd tell me.
well, i'd say back, it's just unfortunate that we live in a world where perfection is misconstrued;
where time bounds mastery,
where .999 is synonymous with 1,
where "good enough" is often sufficient,
where humans are to midas as destruction is to gold,
where it is impossible for many to consider the *possibility* of perfection.

the most beautiful sentiment of love,
at least in my opinion,
are thoughts, portrayed as language, portrayed as communication.
but i sit here, writing this, frustrated.
language is the complex art that separates man from animal.
something we ourselves created,
representative of our own arbitrary forms of expression,
articulation of emotion.
and yet there doesn't seem to be *any* that do you justice.

the basis of each word: each individual phoneme -
contrastingly distinct in essence,
and despite each and every way i string them together,
no blend of sound will ever capture your quintessential ethereal beauty.

each word has been already used.
each word too ordinary.

each word too worn, too simple.
each word's definition tarnished by the constant use of average people.
each word only "good enough",
but this time, insufficient.

i've concluded that no combination will ever constitute
your embodiment of fate at it's finest:
the rare coalition of nature and man,
perfection in my eyes.

how can one's writing,
using
existing,
repetitive,
bland words,
ever amount to indescribable beauty.
it simply cannot.

if i were an artist and you were my subject,
i'd be unable to paint you,
for you're a color only i can decode,
impossible for others to see.
i wouldn't be able to grasp
the true essence of your elegance,
if only given standard colors,
available to everyone else.

i wish you could see yourself from my perspective.
i *also* wish i could create a language unknown to everyone else,
a language only we speak.
for i would shower you with words unavailable to those unworthy,
i would orchestrate a concert with the greatest fusions of sound,
i would put your perfection,
a concept foreign to those who haven't met you,
into words capable of living outside of the depths of my
little red notebook.

thought #1

i wonder what it feels like to fall in love.

        i also wonder why the fear of judgment outweighs
        the ability of confessing one's truest emotions.

i wonder if the possibility of temporary embarrassment reigns supreme
over amplifying our thoughts
to the one we're thinking of
in situations where we're unsure.

            i wonder if the feeling of true love outweighs
            that fear of judgment,
            that possibility of temporary embarrassment,
            those odds of rejection,
            or if it just obliterates that stupid heiarchy of logic altogether.

i wonder if it's because in true love
lies certainty,
rather than confusion.

thought #2

how do you know when you're in love? and *when*? what even constitutes love anyway?

what constitutes love?

if serotonin was tangible,
mine'd lay in the palms of your hands.
descendent of aphrodite,
are you?
for as i take time to analyze the depth of your features,
your beauty still does not compute.
looking at you my vision's impared,
kaleidoscopic illusions,
i'm stunned by the view of you.
in all absence of light,
you'd glow;
putting stars that freckle the night sky to shame.
you're an artist,
your medium: the natural radiance from within you.
i wish my words would paint the way you make me feel,
for it'd be the perfect blend of all that is light in this world.
you're the color of sherbert sunset,
yet if we ran in the rain the water'd run clear,
for no hue would risk draining from you.
if you're a flower,
i'm a bee - in search of your nectar,
drunk on the desire to impress.
you are a face of reassurance in the presence of fear,
comfort - an enticing remedy to a wounded soul.
come lie with me in the middle of the street,
i ask you.
you can admire the sky, i can admire you.
the darkness of night will emphasize our true state:
hanging in the cosmos, the ultimate void of the unknown;
yet sometimes the incomprehensible reveals *utmost* understanding.
we realize we are minute personas enveloped within the large scale of life,
still susceptible to undesired realities.
i wish we were untouchable,
unable to fall victim to the rushed pace of life.
yet time and space have stalled,
did you do that?
our lives finite but our love eternal,
not even time can bound this feeling.
if we only live once, i want to live once with you.

thought #3

i assume that falling in love
must feel like that feeling
when you look yourself in the mirror
and remind yourself that you are actually
very much alive and present in *that* current moment;
like you see yourself,
but more deeply,
in a new sense of rejuvenation,
like you are seeing yourself for the first time;
as if you've opened up a third eye
with the sole purpose of observing yourself objectively.
a feeling of recognition that we were all placed here
for a reason,
and *that* reason is what *you* make of it;
like you have a predeclared purpose that *you* have the opportunity to define
just by living your life in the way you feel fit.
it's a strange sense of supremacy, i guess,
as if you're in complete control of your destiny;
which we are, as long as we believe it.
so i guess the conclusion to my epiphanic comparison is that
love just acts as a portal to a clearer conscience;
a conscience that is not only capable of grasping our truest reality,
but also encapsulating our truest emotions,
invigorating our greatest fantasies,
reminding us that we're not just *us*,
we're human
and we're *all* human
and we're truly a difference in the world;
reminding us that when an opportunity presents itself,
we must embrace it,
and life *itself* is an opportunity
so it will be what we make of it;
reminding us that we are seen,
and our feelings are real,
in the same way love does.

or maybe not at all, i don't know.

the greatest symphony of emotion

blind to the eye,
yet evidently visible to the soul,
that of your aura.

i am enthralled;
wallowing in the
passionate intensity
of beauty
you generate.

my soul grows porous,
for i hope that if i immerse myself
in the abundance of your light,
i will capture even a little for myself.

i blink.

i am running through an open field
where joy grows plentiful.
i am twirling alongside blossoming flowers,
dancing atop the thickest of grasses;
freedom
grows my infatuation with life.
happiness pours from the densely pigmented sky,
casting shadows on the ground,
warming my skin.
the subtle wind cools it.
i breathe deeply,
inhaling dreams and possibilities.
i now lay amongst the earth,
and close my eyes gently,
a true state of bliss;
at my own desire,
without hesitation,
devoid of fear.
my heart beats euphorically;
i smile, then i
float,
carried by the power of
passion from within.
the earth erupts in sound then;
flower petals sing,

wind whistles,
reeds of grass hum,
trees sway to the sound of the heavens.
i lie in the air,
frozen in time,
comforted by
the greatest symphony of emotion.

i blink.

i am looking at you, smiling.

your aura is contagious,
concentrated with the richness of life.
i wish you were aware
of your power,
of my emotion,
of our natural familiarity.
sometimes ignorance is bliss,
but you're in a state of complete oblivion.
when i am around you,
not only do you hold me in a state of
captivation,
but i feel as though i thrive in your presence.

sitting here with you,
i am set free.

thought #4

does anyone else ever feel like they're just doing everything all wrong?

un-

sometimes i resonate with the prefix un-
since the entirety of our existence is to claim liability for
bringing out the worst
of the already freestanding great.
un- puts his words in their mal forms
in the way my touch evidently
rots the living.
we take our talons and claw at the
*un*defensive
and
*un*able,
acting as oppressors to the
*un*powerful.
imagine having such an
*un*deniably *un*touchable
power
where everything wretches
*un*controllably
in your very presence.
words run from un-
in the way expectations
cripple in my hope.
often it's
hard
for the beautifully woven
intricacies of independent words
to digest the fact that
something so seemingly innocent
in nature:
two separate letters conjoined,
can be so
*un*sympathetic
and hostile
as to ruin the entire trajectory of their definition.

thought #5

my eyelashes are going to be so long
if crying makes them grow.

the ocean of life

i am drowning in my own potential,
possible fate, my most daunting endeavor.

are my aspirations too perilous to execute?

still water does indeed run deep,
for the subtle art of deception,
the cost of my life.

do not underestimate the appearance of
ethereal beauty,
for in truth,
lies a treacherous beast within.

i've passed the point of no return.
i flail my arms pathetically,
a last ephemeral attempt of survival.

i can't help but to drown,
for i am suffocated by
the unexpected weight
of my own flawed ambition.

water engulfs my lungs,
my body grows weak;
for what is possibility,
when there is pressure.

i can't flaunt triumph if i'm dead.

light blue subaru

you've taught me that
within oneself,
consistency
creates a
structured security;
the key to the
compelling lock
that is
self identity.

i can picture

the blue inked,
black cased,
pen
sticking out from above the
second button
of your light blue polo;
the one that makes your eyes pop.

the reclining leather sofa
you nap on,
with your right hand lying on your stomach,
gently moving
up
then
down,
syncopated with your breath.

the sound of your voice,
and the rasp in your laugh,
when you pick up the phone
whenever i call.

you're as dependable as the
light blue subaru
you rave about,
that drives us along the coast by your house.

the evanescent exhilaration of spontaneity
will never compare to the
everlasting presence of comfort,

created by reliability.

a language only we speak: eyes of ethereal beauty

i've come to realize that maybe
words aren't the best portrayal
of emotion after all.

that maybe
some things aren't *meant* to be described,
rather solely observed

and admired.

in testing that theory,
i've attentively studied
the depths of your features.
i'm now familiarized with the truth that

embedded within the depths of your skin is a light
that presents itself whenever i look into your eyes.

this light takes advantage of the permeability of
your diluted blue eyes,
soaring through the transparency,
soaking into my soul.

so majestically innate;
i wonder how something so simple
can hold such divine power.

a gaping window to your soul,
they reveal an exposition of emotion;
my only insight to your most vulnerable truths from within.
i'm happily dazed,

tracing the ink blue outline inwards,
as the rich pigment transforms from opaque to translucent,
the diluted blue crashing into your pupil.

so transparent,
yet so saturated.
i stare.

my skin feels dense
with love,

as i bathe in the inviting warmth
of your gaze.
i feel as though
your eyes
reveal
your illuminating presence
in the most beautiful of ways.

if eyes dictated the purity of the soul,
yours would be of the purest.

scribes to your thoughts
they speak silently;
saying everything,
yet nothing at all.

our eyes say what our lips cannot.

nonverbal,
yet explicitly clear.

thought #6

i love love,

but i'm scared that i've grown dependent on it.

thought #7

i wonder if you realize you've become exactly what i told you i feared you'd become.

do we feel distant lately?

i now look into your once perpetually spirited eyes,
and see a barren void of emptiness.
i'm looking right at you,
yet your presence has escaped;
i'm uncertain as to where you are.

clouds now cover your once uncontested sunlight,
i guess enough of our sadness has finally condensed.
i can't see past the dense gray burdens
overwhelming your radiance.

we've changed in time, i know.
but i still wish you'd look at me how you used to,
like i was a light,
guiding you through an opaque world.

now i'm the one trapped in darkness.
my growth restricted,
for without light, i wilt;
if slowly approaching death,
how do you expect me to grow?

in time
tears dry,
but trails of sorrow
still claim dominance on my cheeks.
sadly,
our connection is diminishing completely -
a sacrifice to change.

without you here,
there is a draft in the now vacant house
that is my heart.
the essence of your love: unfortunately nomadic,
abandoning the place it once called home.
bitter chills of uncertainty lie
where the warmth of admiration once did.

even the strongest of flames burn out.
engulfed in a pool of wax,
they suffocate.
their downfall: a product they created themselves;

they are the source of their own destruction.
when our flame finally goes out,
the last of our shared emotion vaporizes off the wick,
fading into the forever abyss.
our separation a candle,
victim of its own destruction.
inevitable indifference,
a product we created in change.

i must find
a place where
i can flourish.
a place where
life is ever growing,
and happiness unrestricted.
a place where
the unpreventable chill of faded compassion is unimaginable.
a place where
change is constant,
yet not limiting.
a place that even the most experienced nomadic lovers cannot locate.

i just want to be
all you need and more,
but i can't.
sometimes in time
lies irreversible change.

the burden of time

as i strive for perfection,
i near mediocracy,
for time exacerbates
my ambitions.
in pursuing mastery
failure is inevitable,
i know.
but patience was never a virtue
i embodied well.
why try so hard
to fall just short?
i indulge in my sorrows,
for all that i do
is still not enough.
my flame
of purpose
is dwindling;
i'm nearly burnt out.
i've been rethinking everything lately,
as one who is short of success does.
big risks can lead to big rewards.
but i'm the contrary -
left questioning my capabilities.
confusion possesses my senses,
self deprecation tears my mentality apart.
i fail to recognize all i have accomplished,
when it's short of what i set out to do.
disappointment in oneself is the utmost toxic of poisons.
i am jack of all trades, master of none.

i wish to tip over the hourglass of life,
and have a moment to myself.
shed my inhibitions,
in the way a snake abandons skin it has outgrown.
i wish to emerge from my once comforting cocoon,
that now imprisons my ability to fly.
i hope to undress,
stripping away layers of stress,
and anxiety,
to reveal a beautiful soul behind an
overwhelming presence of
vulnerability.

time limits my greatness,
ostracizes my uniqueness,
restricts my growth.
i haven't failed,
i just haven't quite succeeded.

give me some more time.

thought #8

i wish i could go back and do it all again.
i wish i could feel all that i used to.
i wish i knew in those moments that
that would be the peak of all that we were.

thought #9

"find success within failure." - someone must have said this before me

thought #10

acceptance might just be the hardest and utmost humbling task in life.

the unknown doorway to heaven: a dream of mine, or rather, a nightmare

nearly four years ago,
you were ten.

you stand in the foyer of our house,
bundled,
in your then favorite
navy blue columbia puffer jacket.

your khaki trousers are too large on you,
but you're comfortable,
and warm,
so you don't care.

you wear those square,
black rimmed glasses,
that covered a good portion of your face.

your hair has gel in it,
combed back,
the way it always used to be.

you clutch your camo luggage,
the one you wished to travel the world with.

when i walked over to see you,
your face lit up.
you admired me in a way that i miss.

your adorable,
adolescent voice
would sing.

i still hear it ringing in my ears.

you look at me like i could do no wrong in your eyes.
you start to speak to me,
when mom asks if you're all ready to go.

my heart suddenly pounds erratically.

NO, it sensed.
NO.

NO. NO. NO.
wait. WAIT.
STOP.
my intuition helplessly alarming my conscious,
yet i can't speak for some reason,
i stay observing.

you start rolling your luggage,
then stop,
drop your hand,
and run into my arms.

"goodbye."
you smiled big.

your hands can't even wrap fully around my body
because you're so little.

mom grabs your hand,
and looks at me,
a tear trailing down her cheek.

your innocence was refreshing,
but evidently overbore your senses.

you wave at me,
still all bundled up,
in your favorite outfit.

NO.

suddenly everything went silent.

i screamed.
i yelled.
i kicked.
i cried.

dad had to hold me back.
i hated him in that moment.

mom escorted you through the door.
i hated her in that moment.

"why are you *doing* this?" i weeped.

"i love you," i heard faintly from the depths of the doorway.
that's actually the last thing i heard.
then the door shut,
and you were forever in the doorway's control.

i cried,
and cried,

and cried.

i layed on the wood floor in our foyer for hours.
my head pressed into my forearms,
digging into the floor.

my body too limp,
my heart too broken,
my desire too weak,
to get up.

you poor thing, you.

you didn't even know what was happening,
where you were going.

we knew what you didn't.

i knew in that moment you were gone forever.
but you didn't.

i knew i'd never see you again.

wherever you are,
i hope you're happy,
i hope you're at peace,
i hope that jacket still keeps you warm,
i hope your trousers are still too loose,
i hope you got to travel the world.

we will meet again,
i promise.

regret

i never thought i'd want to
hold him in my arms forever.

run my fingers through his coarse,
honey tinted hair.
the hair i used to make fun of.

stare into his rich,
jet black eyes
that revealed the most beautiful,
youthful soul.

admire his perfectly straight smile
that only the purest of joy brought out.

listen to him talk,
and say my name.

drop everything i was doing to be with him,
although i never would.

i would now.
i so wish i could.
but i can't.
because he's dead.

ironic how the then insignificant
becomes the utmost memorable
when the unimaginable happens.

thought #11

you taught me that the duration of your life is irrelevant
as long as you mean something to someone,
and you meant something to me.

your life was short,
but beautiful.

these are not pity words,
i can assure you.

i just wish i told you this then.

slowly dying: when one goes, the other is going

mentally coherent
yet physically incompetent,
you poor thing, you;
fully aware of your own
dwindling;
your own
downfall;
aware of
your own
end.
i wonder if you feel trapped.
i wonder if within you,
the optimist
falls victim to the realist.
i wonder how long a strong mind
can prolong the capabilities of an unable body.
do you live within your thoughts,
within your hopes,
within your mind?
your body skeletal,
your skin wrinkled,
your hand barely able to squeeze mine harder when i tell you
i love you.
i sadly
don't even recognize you anymore.
who is *that*? i point. i stare. i sob.
because
you're no longer the version of yourself
i'll forever see in my mind
when i think of you.

mentally *incoherent*
yet physically competent,
you poor thing, you;
unaware of the poor hand
fate has dealt you.
functioning with no direction;
must be hard:
frantically searching
when you don't know what you're searching for.
i wonder if you remember our laughs.
i wonder if you remember squeezing my hand harder when i told you

i loved you.
i wonder if you remember *me*.
but how could you forget all that is *you*?
without the brain,
you're just the heart
that doesn't even know its own
beat.
you might forget me,
but i'll never forget you.

conceptually speaking,
isn't the essence of life
the avoidance of death?
or is that just surviving;
persisting,
enduring,
existing.
just *being*,
just *resisting*

the ultimate demise.

the essence of life
is *not* the avoidance of death;
rather the brewing blend of
strength
and compassion.
humility
and positivity.
capability
and opportunity.
a true and thorough *impact*.

when did life become
the worse alternative
to death?
when the inseparable
are separated,
and you become
the brain
or
the brawn
rather than
the very much alive.

i'm not ready for you to
not be here anymore.
why must we get old?

thought #12

what's on the other side? will we ever meet again?

in a chaotic mind lies a peaceful soul

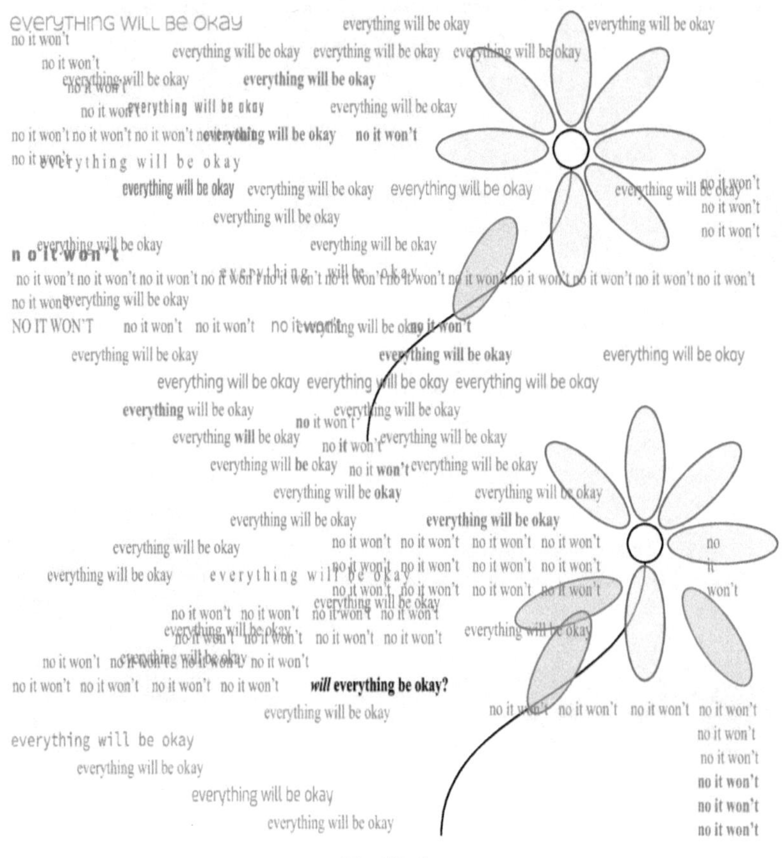

thought #13

i'm not sure if i miss you
or if i miss who you were.

thought #14

"we accept the love we think we deserve." - stephen chbosky

basking in the wake of our grand collapse

cognitive dysfunction,
i malfunction in your presence.
you are still my go to thought,
the ultimate default,
i always resort to you.
your crooked smile,
celestially enchanting,
reverberating
within my head.
gliding steadily,
bumping gently
the sides of my cranium,
synchronized to the beat of my pulse.
i wonder if you think about me
as much as i think about you.
i'm unsure.

i wish for you to be as transparent
as your eyes once were,
for i'm unsure if my love,
so evident,
is reciprocated
or unrequited.
slowly
fearing,
fighting,
flooding,
fraying,
fading,
failing.
it's over, i know.
our change constant,
yet your growth exponential,
i fear my senses are correct
in you leaving
me behind;
flying blind,
right beside
the weight of my
broken heart.
but i refuse
to succumb

to the scum
that is your constant dismissal.

i wither
in your distress.
coming to terms with reality,
i'm a mess:
a savage devouring me
from the inside out.
i wish you would have just
sharpened the blade and impaled me,
rather i'm riven
with aches,
awake
in the wake
of the
deliberately
and
diabolically
sliced
gashes
throughout the entirety of my love.
i'd rather stay here and bleed out,
than continue registering
the concept that despite
all that i've given
and
all that i am
and
all that i forever will be,
you will never love me,
how i love you.
and yet here i still lie,
lost in the labyrinth
of your lackluster love.

allow me to
suppress my discomfort.
bottle up the emotions,
and press them down,
deep,
where they're nearly impossible to access,
for i want to avoid my
pining,

penning,
whining,
wanting
you
to pick me up and tell me you love me,
shower me in compliments,
tell me everything will be okay,
put me first;
to laugh,
smile,
look
at me
the way you once did.

now stopped in time i think.
voices hang in the air,
life moves on,
but i'm stuck,
paralyzed.
in need of a scream,
in need of a release
of pent up,
raw
emotion,
in need of you.
but i forgot,
my voice is suppressed by the static,
i'm a mute.
my body,
rigidly idle,
yet my heart,
free falling.
but don't come back into my life and catch it,
and save the day like how you once did.
give it time to hang in the air,
then let it shatter
so that later on,
i can
bend down on my knees
and collect all of the
demolished pieces of past passion,
and convince myself
that i can piece them back together
as new.

if your life a book,
you're the most unbearable protagonist ever.
to you,
nothing is as trivial
as my effort
to love you.
ignore me again,
maybe this time i'll leave for good,
travel to the
fountain of youth,
and bathe,
baste,
drink,
taste;
a purgatorial attempt
to cleanse off the burden of time
you placed upon me.
this water medicinal,
i'm healed,
maybe i'll now be forever young;
unlimited attempts to
recreate
a better version of
what you currently
hate,
about me.

thought #15

i would say that
i assume heartbreak
must feel like that feeling
when you remember you are actually living in a world you must leave one day,

but i unfortunately don't have to assume.

your petals of the brightest, your scent of the sweetest

after that day,
i will forever despise the
pleasant aroma
that roses emanate;
for i will always associate the scent
with a sudden truth
that broke me.

the brilliant vibrance of velvet
that petals possess
will eventually face a wave of
overwhelming fragility,
encapsulating the stark realization
that inevitably,
dark,
shriveled desperation
takes its place.

even the most supreme
sentiment of love,
essence of life,
echanthing of fragrance,
faces the false hope
of immortality.

watching
you
wither
is
exhausting.

but i'm aware now;
repulsion
is just the fragile
absence
of past admiration.

i just can't stomach the
nauseating stench,
that is

losing you.

thought #16

i'm scared that my current reality
is the unfolding
of everything i feared to be true.

i hoped that my predictions wouldn't manifest themselves,
but i think they have.

a dedication to my younger self:

i was told once that a life
can not be lived
without integrity.
the capacity of that i guess
is up for interpretation;
but subjectively,
i've determined that
it connotes an underlying purpose
that you subtly acknowledge
whenever you carry out
anything
and everything;
of any scale,
at any time.
so, within this frame of mind,
i want to make it explicitly clear
that my biggest goal
is making you proud;
you are my
purpose.
i hope you look at me
and are proud of who we've become.
i hope you look at me
and see everything you've ever wanted to be and more.
i hope my smile
still carries genuine happiness in the way yours did.
i hope though,
that i'm always honest with you,
the way we always have been with each other.
i hope you know
that we won't always see life in ultra saturation
in the way you once did.
i hope you know
i fear
falling short of our potential,
my inability to grow,
that i won't become the person you've always wanted to be,
that you were the peak of my life,
that nothing will ever be the same,
that i've become a burden,
that trying my best is no longer enough.
but most of all,

i fear letting you down.
but of all the hopes,
and all the fears,
i do find comfort in knowing that i *am* living,
because i exude a life of integrity,
knowing that
i have a purpose
of living for you and
forever through you.

thought #17

i don't always laugh because things are funny.
i don't always laugh because i'm a "naturally happy" person.
i don't always laugh because i have nothing going through my head.

so i often wonder why i laugh so much.

i wonder if laughing convinces the depths of myself to be less broken.
i wonder if laughing gives other people the confidence i wish i had.
i wonder if laughing is just i reflex i have to mask anxiety.

thought #18

is childhood sweetest because it comes first?

who am i really?

"no one can make you feel inferior without your consent."[1]
thank you eleanor,
your words *are* wise;
but in some aspects
flawed,
for the enticement of extrinsic approval
lures me tight within its grasp.
did you consider that consent can be exploited by insecurity?

i bet people think
i'm a people pleaser.
i guess objectively you can say i am,
but personally
it's hard to feel satisfied
when nothing *i* do will ever be enough,
if my own validation
doesn't equate
that of others.

...

it's strange that i'm one person,
but i'm a million different people;
all dependent on perspective.

  it's strange that the entirety
  of my identity is the
  fermenting coalition of a
  myriad of slightly different versions of myself.

is it strange though,
that of all the versions that i could possibly see,
i'd wish to see myself from your perspective?

  i wonder if my eyes
  leave my soul vulnerable
  for your interpretation.
  i wonder if they leak despair
  involuntarily.

i wonder if my face
is caked with

the uncertainty
of the impending tomorrows.
i wonder if jealousy
paints a frown on it.

      i wonder if i've accidentally closed an opaque door
      prohibiting transparency between us,
      because
      i sense your distance lately.
      i wonder what you're thinking.
      i wonder, i overthink, i care.
      i wonder if you know i care.

but i wonder,

is
      intimidation
a reflection
      of insecurity?
is
      jealousy
a presence
      of self doubt?
is
      love
truly devoid
      of all hatred?
is
      acceptance
the product
      reflection?

often the truth is
unseen within,
a twisted representation of
reality.
but do you see through that?
do you see the real me?
i wonder what version of myself
you see.
i wish i knew.
but deep down i *know* that
you see the best in me,
because that's just who you are.

i so desperately wish that
i could see myself from your perspective.
i wonder if i'd recognize who i saw.

so who am i really?
i guess that's up for interpretation.
but i think i would like your version of myself best.

[1]quote by eleanor roosevelt

thought #19

i often feel like janice, god of duality.
but if i was, why would i choose to display this face?

just one huge paradox

i've been thinking lately.

just about how many contradictions
are woven into the dense fabric of my identity.

people actually tell me i think too much,
which yes,
i am doing it right now.
but aren't our thoughts the basis of who we are?

to be enveloped in the true depths of one's thoughts,
is to be enveloped in the true depths of oneself.

conceptually speaking,
aren't we all just our thoughts,
portrayed as physical beings?
in conjunction with our souls,
obviously.
unless our thoughts are means to the soul,
then i don't even know.

so it's a good thing right?
to think?
unless it's excessively.
everything in moderation i guess.

thought #20

i think that hardships,
as lame as they are,
create stronger people with stories to tell.
they're the spice to life
that bland people envy.

i hope that by the end of my life
i'll have enough stories to write a book.

thought #21

"set fire to the rain." - adele

ACKNOWLEDGEMENTS

I have so many people to thank, and I would like to express my gratitude to everyone who was involved in truly bringing this idea to life.

In no particular order, I would like to extend my appreciation.

Thank you to all who have taken the time to read this book, and to anyone who relates to the written content. I, myself, can attest that I certainly relate to the protagonist in many ways, and I would like to disclose that the origins of this book root back to a journal I kept as a form of therapy for my most true emotions. If you relate to this book in any way, your feelings are valid and you are most certainly not alone.

Thank you to my family, for allowing me to read them each individual poem throughout the penning process, and for continuing to support and inspire me in all of my aspirations.

Thank you to my eighth grade English teacher, Mr. Putorti, for being the first person outside of my family to read the rough draft of this book and give me feedback. I appreciate your kind words and miss your class greatly.

Thank you to Raul Colón, my uncle and brilliant illustrator, for reading my work and motivating me to continue writing.

Thank you to Carrie Bedard for reviewing my work and for your words of encouragement, and helping guide me through the publication process.

Thank you to Robin Finn for reading three of the original poems and giving me the resources and advice to continue.